Arithmechicks
Add Up

Ann Marie Stephens

Illustrated by Jia Liu

BOYDS MILLS PRESS
AN IMPRINT OF HIGHLIGHTS
Honesdale, Pennsylvania

10 chicks head off to play.
Count their happy beaks.
1–2–3–4–5–6–7–8–9–10.

They cheep and chatter counting
rocks, flowers, and exactly how many
steps it takes to reach . . .

. . . the park!
Over here, over there—
Arithmechicks are everywhere!
These chicks
are ready to add!

2 chicks light plus
3 chicks heavy equals . . .

5 chicks bobbing on a seesaw,
while a lonely mouse watches.

2 chicks far plus
2 chicks near equals . . .

4 chicks playing tag,
while a lonely mouse watches.

5 chicks over plus
1 chick under equals . . .

6 chicks climbing bars,
while a lonely mouse watches.

4 chicks inside plus
5 chicks outside equals . . .

9 chicks hide-and-seeking,
while a lonely mouse watches.

4 chicks fast plus
3 chicks slow equals . . .

7 chicks slipping down a slide,
while a lonely mouse watches.

1 chick in front plus
7 chicks behind equals . . .

8 chicks playing follow the leader,
while a lonely mouse watches.

3 chicks high plus
6 chicks low equals . . .

9 chicks swooshing on swings,
while a lonely mouse watches.

5 chicks on the left plus 5 chicks on the right equals . . .

10 chicks tugging on a rope,
while a lonely mouse watches.

5 • • • • •

All 10 chicks want to play ball.
Scoop it up—

alley-oop,

to the hoop then—

10 chicks stack up—
stretching,
strrrretchiiing—
but not tall enough.

The Arithmechicks
need 2 more inches . . . .

. . . and here they come!

Climbing up the fluff
to reach it,
tap it,

10 chicks tumble down,
plus 1 helpful mouse.

10 chicks line up for home.
Count their fluffy tails:
1–2–3–4–5–6–7–8–9–10,
while a happy mouse waves.

There are many ways to put numbers into groups to get answers or sums, and everyone can have a turn. The Arithmechicks picked the park because addition + play = fun! Here's how you can have fun too: Add up objects around your home, such as pennies, pieces of cereal, or Popsicle sticks. Add up objects in nature such as birds, pebbles, or trees. Just like the chicks, you can write on a notepad or even use a stick to write in the dirt. Adding opportunities are all around you!

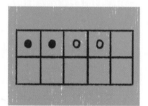

A **number bond** is a picture representation of a number and two parts that make up that number. The large number is the "whole." The two smaller numbers are the "parts" of that whole.

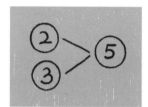

A **ten frame** is a visual tool containing ten squares. The dots represent the two numbers being added to equal the sum. Each set of dots should look different either by color or solid vs. empty.

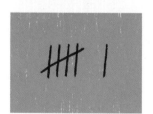

Tally marks are vertical lines that represent the value of each number being added. Every fifth tally mark is drawn slanted, over the previous four marks, making it easier to count by fives. All of the marks in total equal the whole number or sum.

Fingers (or feathers) can be used to add both numbers in an equation. Start on one hand then continue adding up on the other.

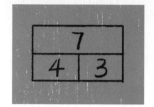

To **decompose** a number or whole means to break it into two parts. These parts, when added together, equal the total of that number or whole. This method is similar to a number bond.

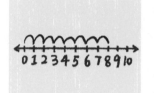

A **number line** is a line of numbers in sequential order. The first number in an equation is the starting point. The second number is added to the first by hopping spaces to the right, equaling the value of that number.

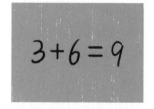

An addition **equation** is a number sentence that shows a plus sign, equal sign, and the numbers that are added together to equal the sum.

To **count on**, start with the first number being added. Then continue to go higher by counting the objects, pictures, or numbers that remain.

For my grade level chicks, who add fun to my life —AMS

Thanks to my family for supporting me so that I can do what I love —JL

Boyds Mills Press • An Imprint of Highlights • 815 Church Street, Honesdale, Pennsylvania 18431 • boydsmillspress.com • Printed in China
ISBN: 978-1-62979-807-3 • Library of Congress Control Number: 2018962346 • First edition • 10 9 8 7 6 5 4 3 2 1
Design by Barbara Grzeslo • The text is set in Futura Medium. • The illustrations are done digitally, and the artist made textures by hand to apply in the digital illustrations.